W9-BON-010

David Wojtowycz

ELEPHANT JOE, Brave Knight!

A tale of knightly chivalrousness.

Random House ⌂ New York

It was a sunny day at the castle.
Elephant Joe and Zebra Pete
were swimming in the moat.
Suddenly a cry came from the castle.

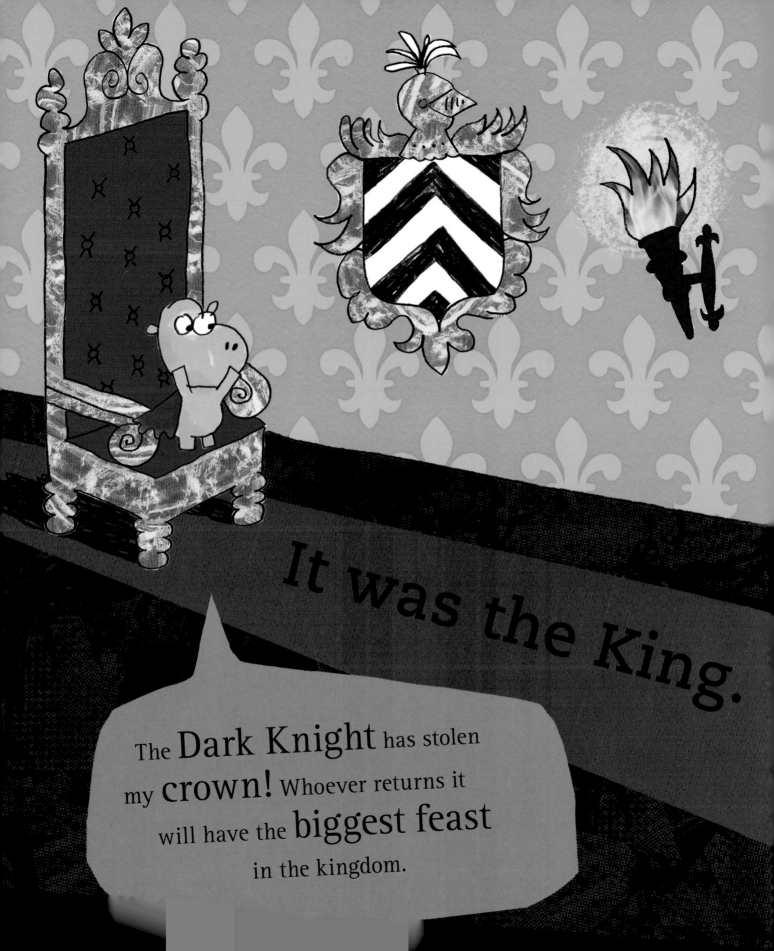

It was the King.

The **Dark Knight** has stolen my **crown!** Whoever returns it will have the **biggest feast** in the kingdom.

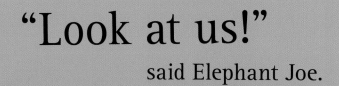

"Look at us!"
said Elephant Joe.
"We're knights!
We shall fight the Dark Knight
and rescue the King's crown.
Giddyup!"

They set off immediately.

Soon they were in the
**Enchanted
Forest.**

The dragon's fire melted
Elephant Joe's sword.

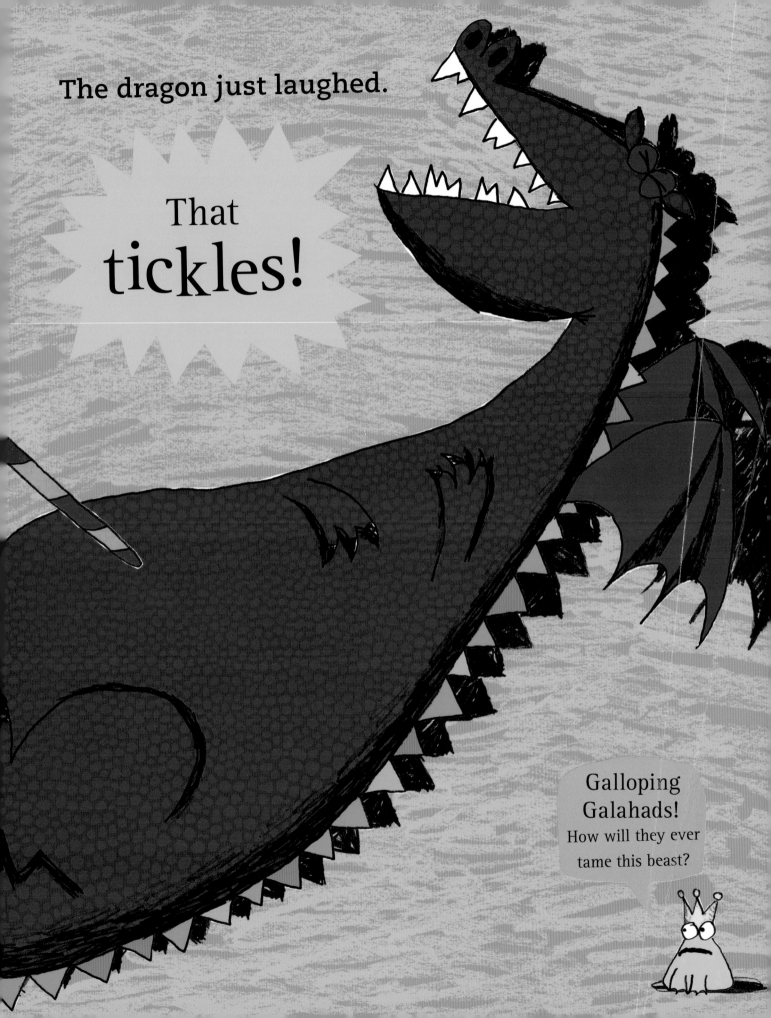

The dragon just laughed.

That
tickles!

Galloping
Galahads!
How will they ever
tame this beast?

Then Zebra Pete said,

Can you let us past, **please?**

"Please"?

No one had ever said "please" to the dragon before. He let them past.

But the damsel was actually . . .

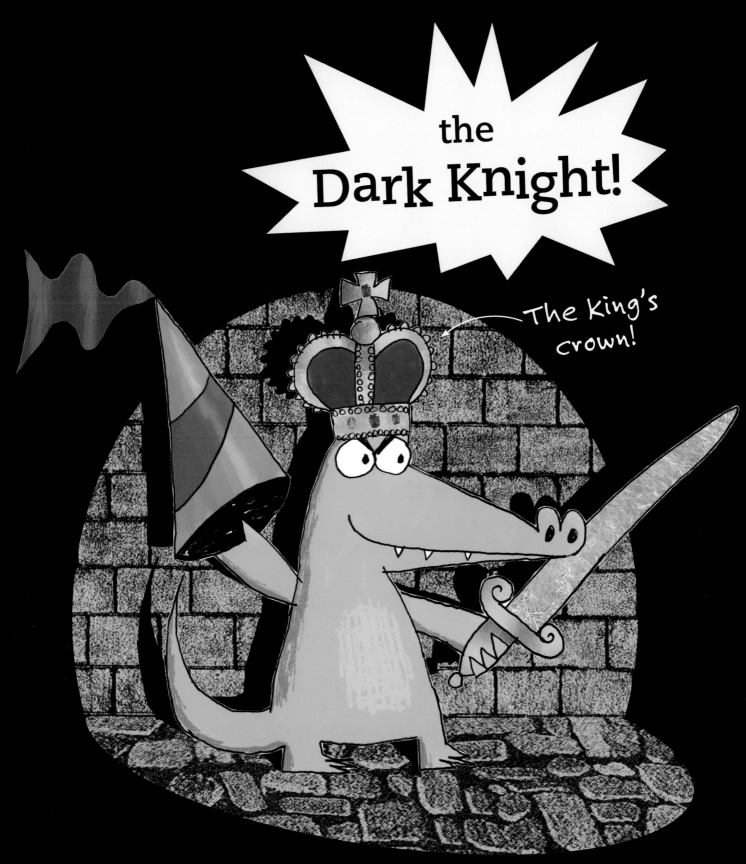

the
Dark Knight!

The King's crown!

Let us out!
We have to defend the King!

Luckily, the dragon had a spare key.
He let them out . . .

. . . and gave them a ride.

CASTLE

They arrived just in time.

Raise the drawbridge!

As the drawbridge went up, the horse chucked the Dark Knight into the moat. **Splosh!** went the crown into the water.

Quick as a flash,
he dived into
the moat.

He saved the
crown and
dragged the
Dark Knight
ashore.

The King was very pleased
to have his crown back.

Arise,
Sir Elephant Joe!

Arise,
Sir Zebra Pete!
We are most grateful
to you both.

"Good idea," said the King. "But first . . ."

"I like being a knight,"
said Sir Elephant Joe.

To Joe and Zack, from Great-Uncle David

Yuck! You are just a frog after all!

Drat! I thought I was a handsome prince!

The End

Copyright © 2011 by David Wojtowycz

All rights reserved. Published in the United States by Random House Children's Books, a division of Random House, Inc., New York. Originally published in Great Britain as *Elephant Joe Is a Knight!* by Alison Green Books, an imprint of Scholastic Children's Books, a division of Scholastic Ltd., London, in 2011.

Random House and the colophon are registered trademarks of Random House, Inc.

Visit us on the Web!
www.randomhouse.com/kids

Educators and librarians, for a variety of teaching tools, visit us at www.randomhouse.com/teachers

Library of Congress Control Number: 2011927722
ISBN 978-0-307-93087-3 (trade)
ISBN 978-0-375-98090-9 (ebook)

MANUFACTURED IN SINGAPORE
10 9 8 7 6 5 4 3 2 1
First American Edition

Random House Children's Books supports the First Amendment and celebrates the right to read.